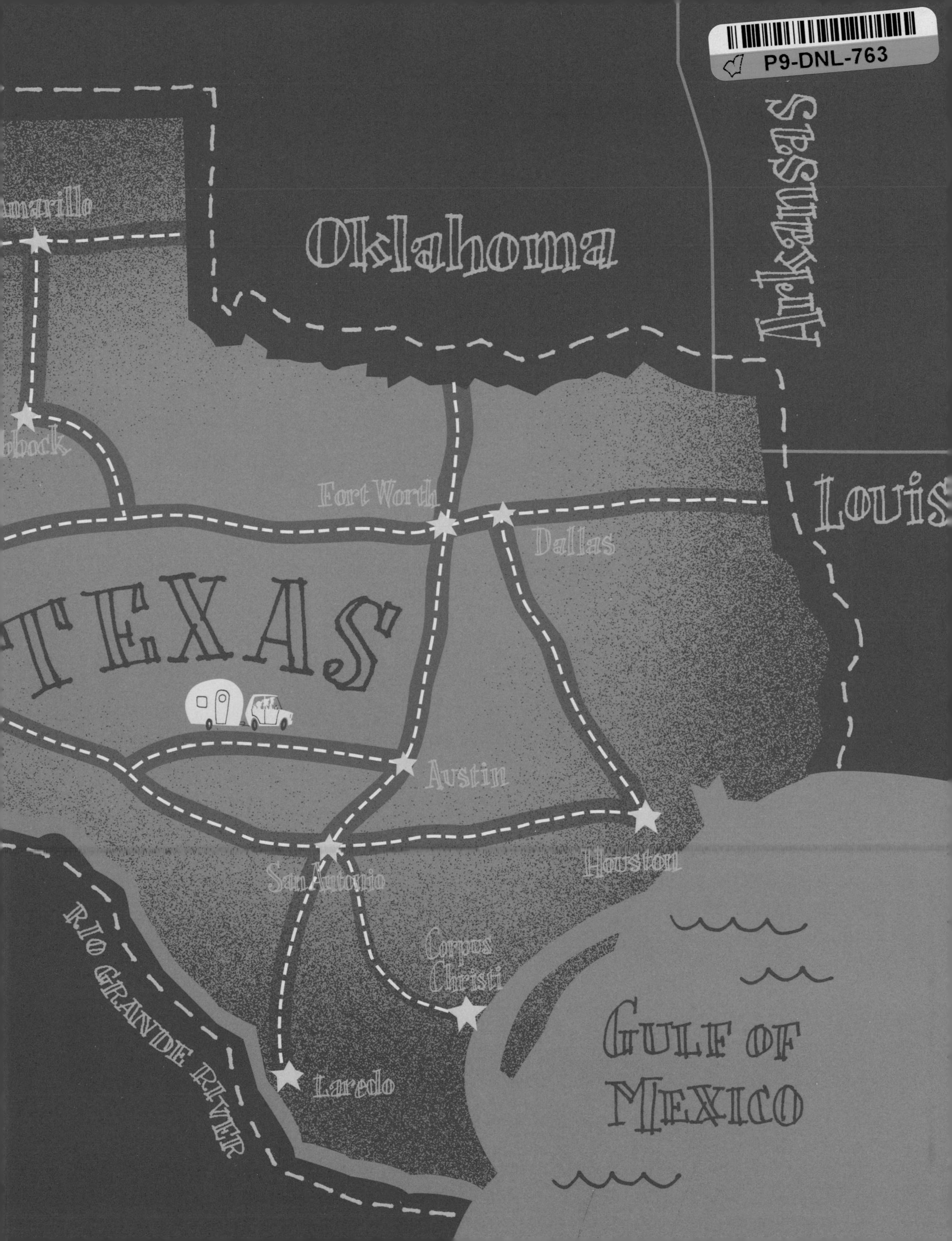
Oklahoma
Arkansas
marillo
bbock
Fort Worth
Dallas
Louis
TEXAS
Austin
Houston
San Antonio
Corpus Christi
Laredo
RIO GRANDE RIVER
GULF OF MEXICO

Larry Gets Lost

in

TEXAS

Illustrated by John Skewes
Written by Michael Mullin and John Skewes

SASQUATCH BOOKS
SEATTLE

The authors wish to thank Katherine Quan and Keith Rosen for their valuable assistance.

Manufactured in China by C&C Offset Printing Co. Ltd. Shenzhen, Guangdong Province, in September 2010
Published by Sasquatch Books
Distributed by PGW/Perseus
16 15 14 13 12 11 10   15 14 13 12 11 10 9 8 7 6 5 4 3 2 1

Book design: Mint Design
Book composition: Sarah Plein

Library of Congress Cataloging-in-Publication Data is available.

ISBN-13: 978-1-57061-680-8
ISBN-10: 1-57061-680-9

www.larrygetslost.com

SASQUATCH BOOKS
119 South Main Street, Suite 400
Seattle, WA 98104
(206) 467-4300
www.sasquatchbooks.com
custserv@sasquatchbooks.com

This is **Larry**. This is **Pete**.

They like riding **together** in the backseat.

The family loved going to Adventurous places.

This new one was all about Wide-open spaces.

New Mexico

U.S.

MEXICO

★ El Paso

Big Bend

TEXAS
"Texas" comes from a Native American word for "friendship," which is the state motto.

RIO GRANDE RIVER
The Rio Grande forms the border between the United States and Mexico. It is the fourth-longest river in the U.S.

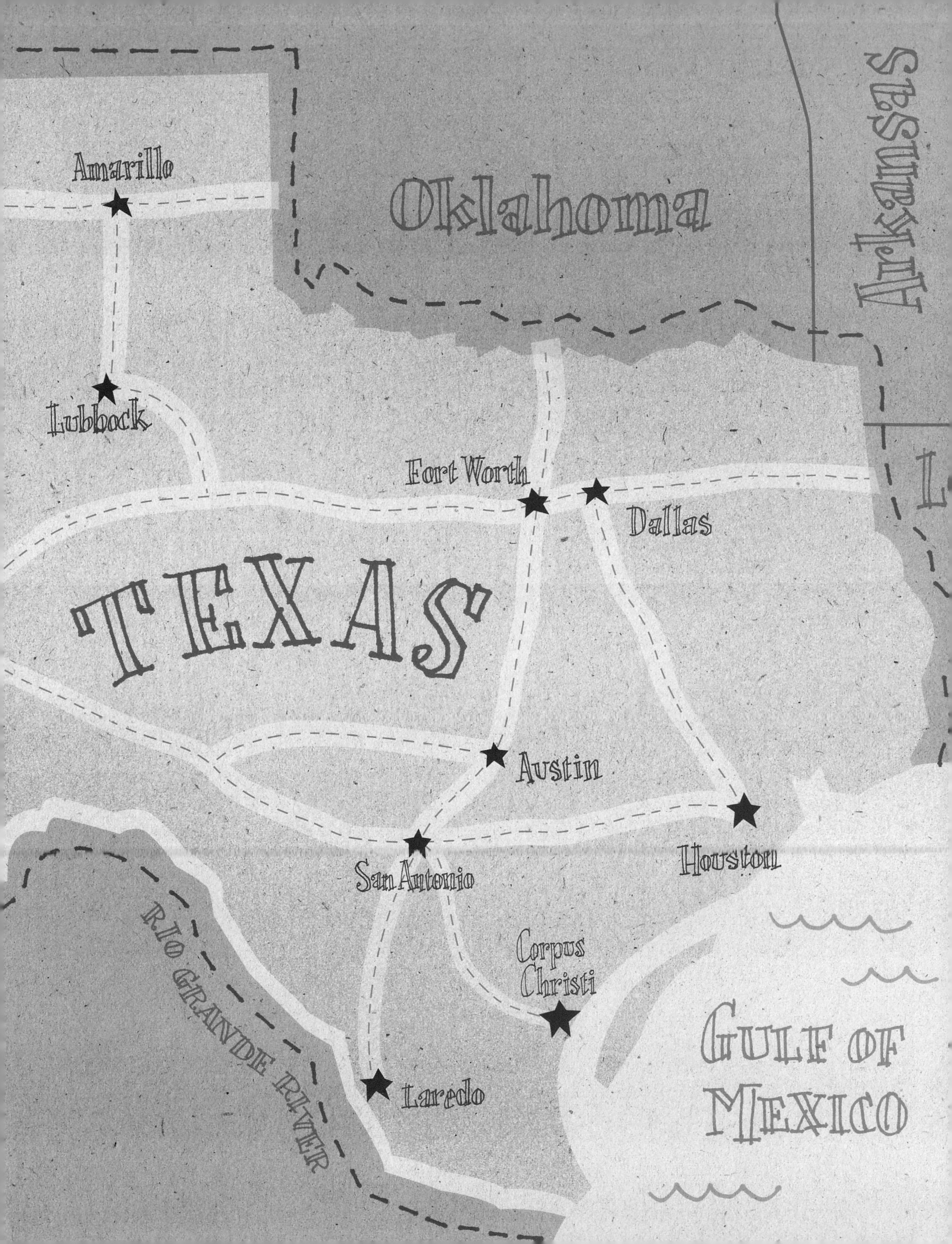

Amarillo

Oklahoma

Arkansas

Lubbock

Fort Worth

Dallas

TEXAS

Austin

Houston

San Antonio

Corpus
Christi

RIO GRANDE RIVER

Laredo

GULF OF
MEXICO

EL PASO

At the first stop there was a hill,
And on top was a star.

Then the **biggest** boots
Larry had seen, by far!

ROCKETBUSTER BOOTS
Home of the largest pair of real leather cowboy boots in the world (size 328-D)!

WEST TEXAS

They drove a long while
Through a curious place.
At first it looked empty,
But that wasn't the case.

CHIHUAHUAN DESERT
The largest desert in North America, it extends from
Mexico to New Mexico, Arizona, and Texas. Can you
see the animals that live in the desert?

While Pete ate with his parents
At a picnic spot they'd found,
Larry stayed in the **trailer**
With the windows rolled down.

Larry's **hunger** was something
He never could hide.
And a tangy smell swirled
Through the air just outside.

It was some kind of meat
On a sauce-covered bun.
He could get it and **eat it**
Before Pete was done.

Larry made his decision
And pounced on his treat,
But there was so much food,
It took a long time to eat.

His tummy full,
He came up gasping for air,
And saw that his best friend Pete
WASN'T THERE!

Back on the ground
Was a strange little guy
Who walked right up to Larry
As if to say: "Hi."

His outside looked hard
Like a rock or a shell,
But he could offer no help
From what Larry could tell.

THE NINE-BANDED ARMADILLO
Native only to the southern U.S.
(primarily Texas), this small animal has
a leathery armor shell. "Armadillo" is
Spanish for "little armored one."

Larry searched the whole lot
Not once, but **twice,**
'Til he saw a trailer with a creature
Who seemed very nice.

Without Pete
Larry had no clue what to do.
Then his friend nodded as if to say:
"There's room for **you,** too."

Riding in comfort, Larry thought
"What a lucky day!"
But Pete and his parents
Had gone the **opposite** way.

Larry saw **cars** like **trees** sticking out of the ground . . .

CADILLAC RANCH
This outdoor sculpture was created in 1974 by
burying 10 real Cadillacs in the desert.

. . . While at a huge park
Pete's **pup** wasn't around.

BIG BEND NATIONAL PARK
Named for a "big bend" in the Rio
Grande, this 800,000-acre park
includes mountain, river, and
desert environments.

RODEO
TONIGHT

Larry stopped in a place
Where the **whole town** goes,
And he saw his new friend
All dressed up in **fine** clothes.

Almost everyone there
Wore the same kind of hat,
But not one of them knew
Where **Pete** was at.

Rodeos are popular year-round in Texas. Sporting events are based on the skills required by working cowboys and include roping, steer wrestling, bronco riding, and barrel racing.

On his search Larry saw
Some pretty **strange** birds.
It was hard to find proper
Descriptive words.

Some big ones were **eating**
At a steady pace . . .

PUMP JACKS

Oil has been a huge part of the state's economy since it was discovered in 1901, near Beaumont. Pump jacks, or oil derricks, pump up and down all day and night and are a common sight in Texas.

WIND FARMS
Texas produces more wind power than any state in the U.S.

AUSTIN

. . . While **"scary"** ones swooped
Around another place.

CONGRESS AVENUE BRIDGE
In the summer, about a million bats live under the bridge. People gather at sunset to watch the bats wake up and fly out to hunt for their evening meal of insects.

PALACE BEACHWEAR AND GIFTS

ORION'S BELT
These 55-foot-long stainless steel weather vanes turn with the wind.

Pete, Mom, and Dad arrived at a shore
With a ship museum and lots to explore.

Two **sculptures** pointed west. Was that a clue
That might lead the family to **you-know-who?**

USS LEXINGTON
An aircraft carrier launched into service in 1943, it served in the
Pacific Ocean during World War II and is now a floating museum.

Lots of people were at
An **old building** of stone
But Larry didn't see Pete.
He was still all alone.

THE ALAMO

The Alamo was originally a mission, but is most
famous as the site of a battle in 1836 during the
Texas Revolution. The Texian soldiers' battle cry
was "Remember the Alamo!"

While watching people
Shop and eat
Larry heard a voice
That sounded like **Pete's.**

He looked around
Here and there,
But didn't see him
Anywhere.

RIVER WALK
The San Antonio River passes through
the middle of the city; the Walk is a
popular place to eat and shop.

Johnson Space Center

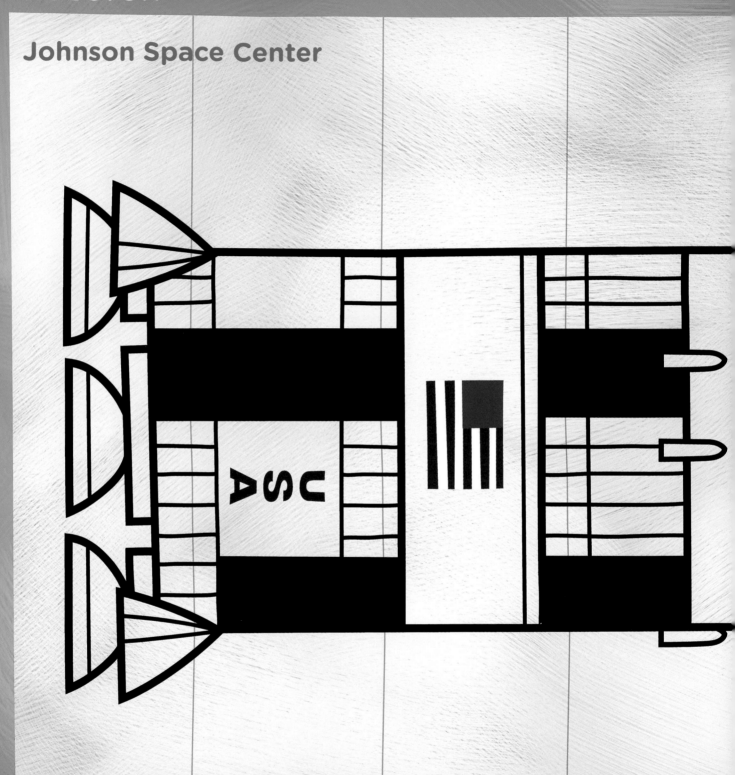

Pete and his folks visited an **amazing** place,
With a big rocket for flying to **outer space!**

SATURN Ⅴ

ROCKET PARK
The Saturn V Rocket is the largest rocket
ever built and was the type used to
fly people to the moon.

Pete learned about the training that **astronauts** do
He only wished **Larry** could have learned this stuff, too.

HOUSTON

And later, nearby
In a **bustling** town,
Pete didn't see Larry
While he was walking around.

HOUSTON TUNNEL SYSTEM
There are more than 6 miles of tunnels under the city. On hot days, more people are underground in the air-conditioned tunnels than on the sidewalks.

FORT WORTH

FORT WORTH STOCKYARDS
The stockyards are a former livestock market where cowboys used to deliver cattle after cattle drives.

TEXAS LONGHORN
A breed of cattle known for its enormous horns. The horns can sometimes reach 7 feet, tip to tip.

In a quieter place,
Larry thought all hope might be lost.

'Til he was stopped by a man
Whose path he had crossed.

The man was dressed in cowboy gear.
He took Larry's collar and said "Let's lookie here . . ."

The cowboy drove Larry
To yet **another** city.
The places they passed
Were exciting and pretty.

A flying **red** horse
Was quite a neat trick,
And one building looked
Like a **lollipop** stick.

BIG TEX
Since 1952, this 52-foot-tall character has been welcoming people to the State Fair by talking and waving his hand.

Larry came to a **huge** fair
That was jam-packed and loud.
How would he ever
Find **Pete** in this crowd?

There was **music**
And all kinds of **food,** end to end.
But he had to stay focused
And look for his friend.

When a **GIANT** said
"Howdy folks!"
And pointed the way . . .

. . . Larry ran up to Pete,
And they both yelled:
HOORAY!!!!!

CONTENTS

GEE WHIZ!

Pee is a part of our daily lives. And that's a *GOOD THING.*

Imagine what would happen if we didn't pee. All that water and milk, juicy fruit and soup, building up and up until . . . well, it's best not to think about that.

Let's just say that **PEE CAN SAVE YOUR LIFE—** in more ways than one.

Nowadays they use chemicals instead, but not long ago, drug companies used a part of our pee to make medicine. This substance, called urokinase, helped dissolve the blood clots that caused heart attacks.

Pee also gives warning about another kind of attack. While out with their cattle at night, Maasai herdsmen in Africa sometimes wake to what seems like a rainstorm. This downpour is actually the sound of their *ENTIRE HERD* peeing at once. The cattle's fear tells the herdsmen that a lion is about to strike.

In 1815, Captain James Riley and the crew of the *Commerce* were SHIP-WRECKED off the coast of Africa. To get back home, they had to cross the very hot, very dry Sahara Desert. When they ran out of water, they survived by drinking camel urine.

WE DON'T TALK ABOUT IT MUCH, BUT PEE IS PRETTY AMAZING.

HOW AMAZING?
READ ON....

PEE BASICS

The watery part of food and drink makes a LONG JOURNEY before it passes out of your body as urine. It is absorbed into your bloodstream first. Your heart pumps this blood around and around your body, passing it through your kidneys at each turn.

In fact, 400 gallons of blood pass through an adult's kidneys each day, and about 150 gallons for a ten-year-old kid. The kidneys pull out waste products, salt, and about a quart and a half of water a day. This SOON-TO-BE PEE then travels to its storage tank—the bladder. Kids' bladders can hold an ounce or more for every year of their age. Adult bladders can store up to 2½ cups of urine. But they feel the urge to pee five to seven times a day, whenever they collect about a cup's worth.

Pee is light or dark yellow depending on the amount of water in it. A mellow yellow turns NEON BRIGHT, however, if you take Vitamin B. Beets, rhubarb, and blackberries can turn it reddish brown.

While it's inside you, pee doesn't smell at all. It only gets STINKY after it sits out in the air. Some medicines make your pee smell different. Eating asparagus also gives it a funny odor, although only half of us have the gene that lets us detect that perfume.

Talk about PERFUME— some women in ancient Rome drank turpentine (which can be poisonous!) because it made their urine smell like roses.

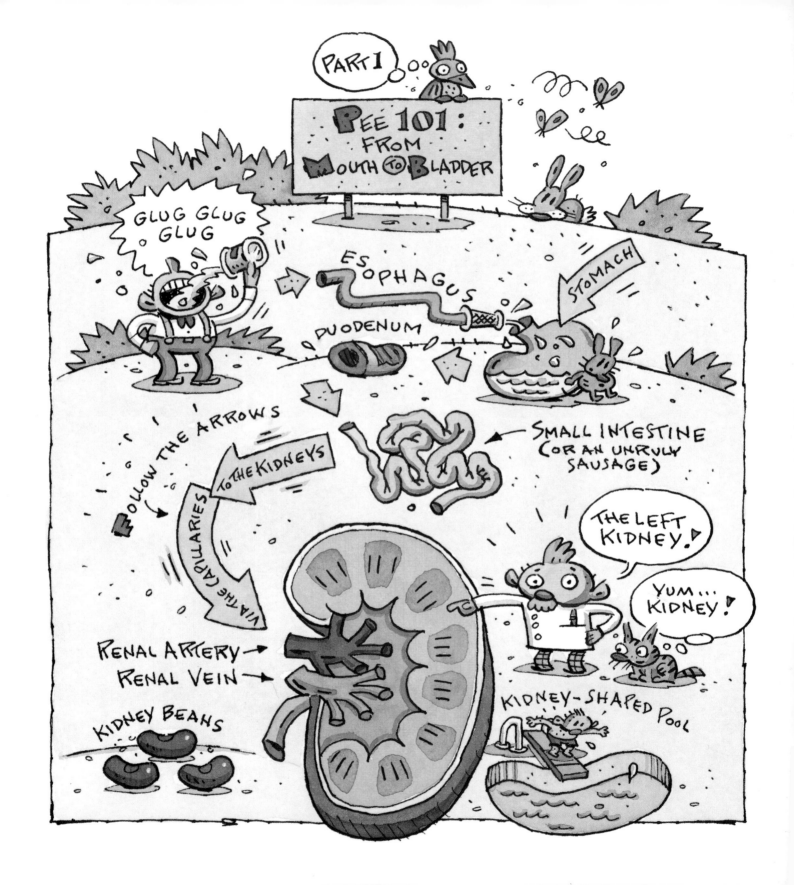

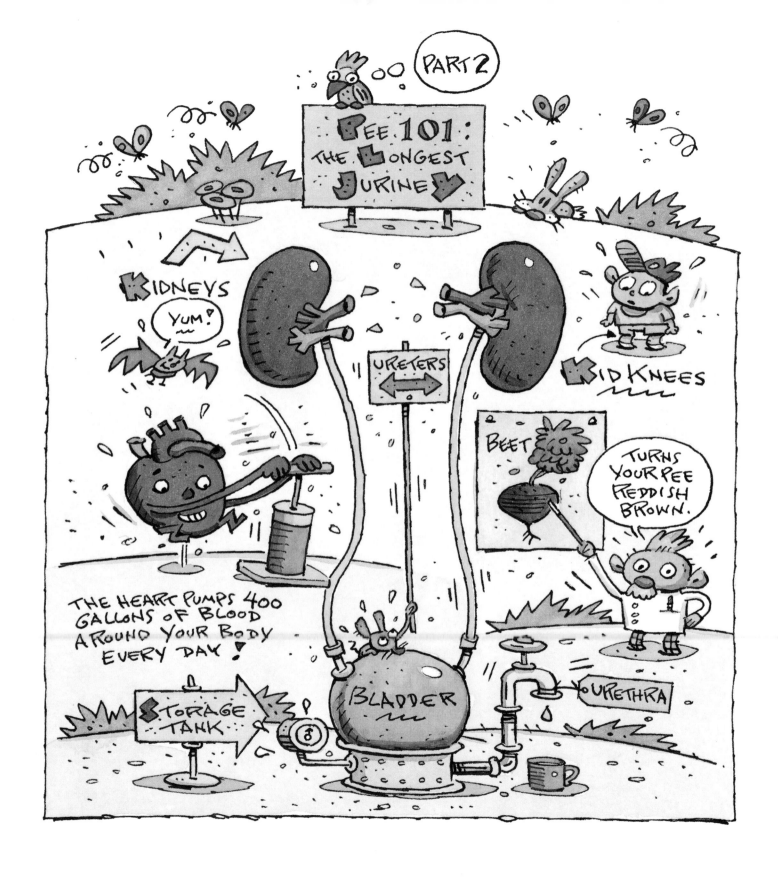

STAND UP AND BE COUNTED

Men stand up to pee and women sit down. Makes sense, given the way our bodies work, right?

NOT NECESSARILY.

In ancient Egypt and Ireland, women stood and men sat or squatted. That's how the Apaches did it too.

In many Muslim cultures, everybody sits or squats. In fact, they think standing up to pee is SOMETHING DOGS DO—not humans.

In ancient China, everyone stood. Chinese noblemen peed into hollow canes so the liquid would flow far from their bodies. You would too if you wore such fancy clothes at court.

Until 200 years ago, European women also peed standing up because of their clothes. They wore long dresses and NO UNDERPANTS. When necessary, they could stand and pee—hopefully outside—without anyone else noticing.

Sometimes standing up to pee is a mistake. Each year, in Canada, about 225 men stand up in a boat so they can pee over the side—and, as a consequence, FALL OVERBOARD and drown.

TO PEE OR NOT TO PEE

NOW THAT IS THE QUESTION!

Some people's jobs make us wonder: How do they manage to pee?

Take YE OLDE KNIGHT in armor, for example. Actually, he didn't have as hard a time as you might think. Wearing a suit of armor was like wearing a short dress, except that it was made of metal and weighed 65 pounds. Its steel plates didn't completely cover his middle. So the knight could pull up his mail skirt and pull down his loosened hose and underwear. He had to be careful, though. The acid in urine could RUST his armor.

Knights dealt with their bathroom emergencies before riding into battle. Fighter-jet pilots don't have that luxury. Flying alone, they cannot dash to the toilet (in fact, there isn't one on board!). Luckily, they have baglike gadgets called PIDDLE-PAKS to pee into while sitting at their controls.

Truck drivers don't have toilets in their eighteen-wheelers either. They could pull into a rest stop, but sometimes they use their own version of a Piddle-Pak instead. They pee into gallon jugs and toss them on the side of the road. During just one month, cleanup crews in Washington State found over 1,000 of these bottles on a 100-mile stretch of highway. And that's not the worst of it. In the summer's heat, pressure builds up inside these jugs—and they can EXPLODE upon contact.

PEEING THROUGH HISTORY

1. PREHISTORY We know ancient people ate bison and woolly mammoth, because they decorated their caves with pictures of their hunts, and anthropologists have found fossilized animal bones in prehistoric *TRASH HEAPS.* Unfortunately early man never painted pictures of where he went to the bathroom— and pee leaves no fossil evidence. So where prehistoric people peed is a bit of a *MYSTERY.* Most likely, they went outside their caves and camps.

Many animals have special toileting areas, from cats and rabbits to llamas and wildebeests. We can only hope that early humans were as sensible.

II. THE ROMAN EMPIRE

Rome brought civilization to the world in more ways than one. In the first century A.D., the city built grand public bathrooms of polished marble. Each toilet had its own bucket of salt water with a *SPONGE* tied to a stick for wiping. People paid to use these bathrooms; then the city made even more money by selling the pee to tradesmen who bleached cloth with it.

Even ancient Rome had its share of *GRAFFITI* artists. So officials posted a warning. They adorned the bathrooms with paintings of gods who would punish anyone who wrote on its walls.

III. EUROPE For more than a thousand years after the Roman Empire fell, Europe went through a bad time toiletwise. Public facilities ranged from none to worse. People on the streets of Edinburgh, Scotland, had to search for the man who patrolled the city with a *BIG BUCKET* and a bigger cloak. For a price, they could use his bucket with the cape draped around them for privacy.

Indoor options weren't much better. In Italy, the artist Leonardo da Vinci proposed that houses be built with spiral staircases so people couldn't pee in the corners.

In Paris, a thousand people could be entertained in the Louvre, the king's palace. But they did not have a single public bathroom to go to. Countesses, dukes, and admirals all peed (and pooped!) in courtyards, hallways, and empty rooms. Meanwhile, the common folk were throwing the contents of their chamber pots *OUT OF WINDOWS* onto city streets. Pedestrians didn't know whether to protect themselves by looking up or watching where they stepped.

No wonder they had a *REVOLUTION.*

IV. THE WHITE HOUSE

In 1776, the United States had *its* revolution. Its goal of equality may have inspired plans for the WHITE HOUSE. The president's plumbing was no better than anyone else's. Even though inventors had started working on toilets by then, the White House was built with only one OUTHOUSE in its backyard.

In 1801, President Thomas Jefferson had two small rooms built, each with a toilet-like device flushed by an overhead tank of rainwater. As time and technology advanced, many toilets were added. For a long time, however, there still weren't enough for all the guests at big dinner parties. After a meal in the late 1800s, gentlemen would go to a private room to smoke cigars and use chamber pots. Women mostly used CONTROL.

Nowadays there are thirty-five bathrooms in the White House. There are also hundreds of people working and visiting there during the day. Don't worry about the president, though. He has his own private bathroom, right off the Oval Office.

V. THE FUTURE

It's nighttime and you stumble toward the bathroom, mumbling a few words to let your toilet know you're coming. It turns on a light to welcome you. And turns off the *VIDEO TILES* on the bathroom wall because you're not allowed to watch late-night TV.

Toilets of the future will be very *SMART.* Recognizing voices, they'll raise their seats for boys and put them down for girls. They'll warm that seat for those who want it. They will even adjust themselves to the perfect height for each visitor.

They will wash and dry you if need be—no more toilet paper. Meanwhile their computers will analyze your pee (and poop) to make sure you're healthy. If there's a problem, they can e-mail your doctor. If you aren't eating enough *FRUITS AND VEGETABLES,* they can e-mail the supermarket to deliver some.

Finally, they will flush on command—kids in the future will have no excuse.

PEES IN A (SPACE)POD

America's first manned space flight in 1961 was only fifteen minutes long. So no one worried about toilets. But delays forced astronaut Alan Shepard to sit in the rocket for hours, waiting for takeoff. After a while, he needed to pee. Badly. Shepard became the first American in space and also the first one to *WET HIS SPACESUIT.*

Eventually astronauts got a space toilet. To use it, they each have their own funnel attached to a tube. They can pee into this funnel, nicknamed *"MR. THIRSTY,"* while sitting or standing, even while floating around. A gentle vacuum sucks the urine into a tank without spilling a drop. This is very important since astronauts aren't the only things that can float around the cabin.

When the tank is full, they shoot the pee outside, where it freezes into clouds of ice crystals that look like *STARS.* Astronaut Wally Schirra liked to call it "Constellation Urion."

One time the pee froze onto the spacecraft. Mission Control was afraid it would damage the ship, but the crew balked at the idea of doing a spacewalk to fix it. No one wanted to be known as the astronaut who *CHIPPED PEE OFF THE SHUTTLE.* Eventually they used the ship's robot arm instead.

Bringing water into space is expensive. So the International Space Station is building a system to purify and reuse the water in pee—and not just human pee. Many animal experiments are conducted on board; NASA estimates that *SEVENTY-TWO RATS* pee about as much as one astronaut.

THE CALL
OF NATURE

Liquid in, liquid out—the idea behind urination seems pretty simple. But different animals do it in very different ways. . . .

When a *VAMPIRE BAT* taps into dinner, it drinks about two tablespoons of blood. Doesn't seem like much, but this feast equals more than half of the bat's body weight. That's quite a load to lift into the air when the bat flies home.

Luckily, the vampire bat's urinary system works overtime. Two minutes after the bat starts drinking, it starts peeing. It drinks and pees and pees and drinks—keeping the nutritious part of the blood while unloading the watery part. By the time the bat is done with its meal, it has already slimmed down enough for *TAKEOFF.*

Bird pee isn't very watery. Having sort-of *SOLID PEE* isn't that important for birds that are flying or perched in trees. But it is the best pee to have when growing inside an egg. For one thing, it takes up less room in the shell. It also does not dissolve so it can't poison the developing chick.

Baby bears are born in the winter and stay inside their dens until spring. Each time the newborn cubs finish nursing, their mom licks their *BOTTOMS* to make them pee. The mother bear then drinks the pee, which keeps their home clean and tidy.

FLOW CHART

Mice are little animals. They don't *DRINK* much—or pee much either. It would take a dozen mice one whole day to fill a tablespoon with pee.

Horses are much bigger. A large one, like a Clydesdale, can pee more than 4½ gallons a day.

Elephants are huge, and they pee *HUGE AMOUNTS*—more than 13 gallons a day. But if you want to double-check this measurement, pick a male elephant to follow around. It would just be easier. Female elephants often poop and pee at the same time.

A fin whale's bladder can hold 5½ gallons of urine. The amount of urine they produce each day, however, is a mystery. When an animal pees into the ocean, it's kind of *TOUGH TO MEASURE.*

DRY RUN

In dry climates, water is so PRECIOUS that animals can't waste a drop. That includes the water in their pee too.

Tortoises in the Mojave Desert get most of their water from eating juicy plants. But it only rains enough for those plants to grow every other year or so. How does the desert tortoise get enough water?

It saves its urine. The tortoise stores that LIQUID GOLD—up to one-third of its body weight—in its bladder. Then, when needed, the water in its pee flows back into the tortoise's body while the waste stays put.

Camels don't actually store water in their HUMPS. When they need to, they keep most of the water in their bodies from becoming pee instead. As a result, their urine becomes twice as salty as seawater. And when they do let go of it, they pee all over their legs. This helps cool them down.

As soon as they find more water, they fill up. Camels can gulp down 25 gallons of it within ten minutes.

PEE POSTINGS

Animals can't read newspapers or use cell phones. So they have to find other ways to communicate. Some use pee to GET THEIR MESSAGE ACROSS.

Lots of male animals pee on the edges of their territory. It's their way of saying, "Keep out, unless you want to fight!" Cats and wolves do it; white rhinos too. In fact, that's one reason dogs keep sniffing the trees in their neighborhood.

This message to "stay away" may help save Africa's wild dogs. As their own territory gets smaller, these animals are wandering onto farms looking for food. Scientists have sprinkled WILD DOG URINE at the edges of the farms. They are making a pee fence, telling the dogs to stay away from angry farmers with shotguns.

DANG!

WILD DOG PEE

Cave rats mark their territory too; they make urine trails throughout the deep caverns they call home. This time, the pee isn't telling others to keep out. It's a *STINKY ROADMAP* that tells the rats how to find their way in the dark.

The South American degu also uses pee to mark its passageways, but smell has nothing to do with it. The urine of this little rodent reflects ultraviolet light, a kind of light we cannot see. Luckily the degu can, so it has *SECRET PEE PATHS* that few other animals can detect.

The Siberian chipmunk uses someone else's pee to send a message—a misleading one. These chipmunks douse themselves with snake pee whenever they can. Smelling like a *SNAKE* (and not a tasty chipmunk) can keep other predators away.

RATS!

WAR AND PEES

Male *HIPPOS* spend a lot of time patrolling their stretch of the Nile River. Sometimes they meet up and have a border war. The hippos turn so they are butt-to-butt. They cover each other with a pee-and-poop combination, twirling their tails like propellers to get plenty at *NOSE LEVEL.* Then they move on, happy to have fought the battle.

Male lobsters *FACE* each other when they decide who rules the ocean floor. Crunching claws are only part of the scuffle. Lobsters' bladders are in their heads, and when they fight, they squirt each other in the face with pee. The loser remembers the smell of his opponent's urine. If they meet up again within a week, just a whiff of that pee tells the losing lobster to back down before he begins.

When lobsters are interested in love, not war, it's the *FEMALE* that makes the first move. She marches over and pees into a male's den, delivering a chemical LOVE LETTER that says, "I'm interested." Most likely he is too, so he rushes out and invites her in.

Using pee to conduct both war *and* romance does seem odd at first. But if you think about it, the pee is just announcing, "Hey, pay attention to me!"

The BILLY GOAT makes sure no one with a nose could miss him. He urinates on his belly and chest, even his beard. He enjoys the smell of his pee perfume and so, he hopes, will all the she-goats nearby.

A male porcupine sprays his perfume in a different direction. After a little NOSE-RUBBING with his lady friend, he douses her with pee. It's an unusual way to be romantic but, if you're a porcupine, HUGGING is not an option.

NATURE'S GOLD MINE

We call it a *WASTE PRODUCT* but . . .

Hunters daub themselves and their dogs with fake raccoon pee to hide their scent from prey.

In winter, some park managers spray their beautiful evergreens with fox pee. The smell is barely noticeable outdoors. But if Christmas-tree thieves ignore the posted signs and bring them inside warm houses, the stink is overwhelming.

What else can you do with a splash of pee? Plenty.

A British bus company uses sheep urine to reduce *CITY SMOG.* A chemical in the pee converts part of fuel exhaust to nonpolluting nitrogen and steam.

People have used pee to remove ink spots. But it can help stain things too. Some cultures mixed pee with coal dust to make dye for their *TATTOOS.* Others used it while dying cotton because it helped colors like the indigo blue of blue jeans stay in the fabric.

People have used pee to cure tobacco.

They have bathed in it to cure their rheumatism.

Some cheese makers used to add a dash to their wares to create a *TANGY FLAVOR.*

AND THAT'S NOT ALL. . . .

PEE P. I.

Pee can be *A CLUE* that solves mysteries. Right now scientists are teaching mice to sniff out the fifty genes in human pee and sweat that make each person smell different from all others. Identifying someone's "odortype" could be a great way to solve crimes. Who needs a witness if a crook leaves his scent behind?

So pee may crack some mysteries, but it has helped create others. Ancient Roman spies used pee as *INVISIBLE INK* to write secrets between the lines of their official documents. (That's where the expression "Read between the lines" came from.) These messages appeared only when heated.

Pee was still part of the *SPY GAME* a few decades ago. A U.S. agent stood in front of a sink washing his hands, waiting for President Brezhnev of the Soviet Union to walk in the restroom. The spy signaled which stall the president used, and fellow spies drained that pipe after the flush. They examined Brezhnev's pee to find out about his health.

URINE THE ARMY NOW

Huge armies create huge amounts of waste. GETTING RID OF IT can be a big job. Sometimes it's better if they don't. . . .

During the Civil War, the Confederacy needed a chemical called saltpeter to make GUNPOWDER. The South didn't have mines where saltpeter could be found, but they did have pee. And a way to make saltpeter out of human urine. So the army put ads in the newspaper asking Southern ladies to save their pee. It also said that "wagons with barrels will be sent around to gather up the lotion."

During World War I, soldiers used their own pee. In April 1915, the German army released poison gas as a weapon for the first time. By May, the Allied armies had invented the first GAS MASKS. Soldiers tied urine-soaked cloths around their noses and mouths. A chemical in their pee gave them a chance to run before the poison hurt them.

Even today pee still comes in handy. To keep soldiers from carrying too much weight into battle, the U.S. army gives them dried food in a pouch. At mealtime, soldiers must put the moisture back in. First choice, water—clean or dirty—the pouch filters out the YUCKY STUFF. But in a pinch, pee will do the job.

PEE M. D.

Doctors have always used urine to diagnose disease. To detect an illness called diabetes, for example, some docs poured pee onto sand to see if it attracted bugs. This idea made sense; diabetes makes urine sweet. That's why other physicians just *DIPPED A FINGER IN* and took a taste.

Today doctors in England are leaving the dirty work to others. They have discovered that some dogs can detect cancer just by smelling people's urine.

Throughout history, people have also used pee to treat illness. Ancient Greek doctors tried curing *MADNESS* with donkey pee. Others tried to get rid of fevers by boiling an egg in the patient's urine and burying it in an anthill.

American pioneers treated earaches by pouring warm urine in their ears and plugging them up with cloth.

Urine really can clean wounds and help prevent infections. Many years ago, part of a *SWORDSMAN'S NOSE* was sliced off at a duel. A doctor snatched it up, peed on it, and sewed it right back on. The nose healed perfectly.

People still use urine as medicine today. What should you do if you're in the ocean and get stung by a jellyfish? Come to shore and pee on the sting. Urine keeps the venom from making you sick.

Millions of folks in Germany, South America, and Asia use this liquid to treat more than jellyfish stings. They drink a glass of their own pee each day. They think it will cure flu, cancer, even baldness.

But the African country of Cameroon doesn't like the idea. In Cameroon, pee-drinking is a crime that can put you in *JAIL.*

PEE SOAP

Nowadays people think of urine as something to wash away, but pee was actually one of our FIRST SOAPS. When urine mixes with air, part of it turns into ammonia—an ingredient in many detergents on grocery store shelves.

The Pilgrims didn't have supermarkets in their America, so they made CHAMBER LYE instead. They let their pee sit in a barrel and then mixed it with ashes. On washday, the ammonia in their chamber lye cut through greasy stains. Another chemical in the pee acted like bleach, making clothes bright and clean. Don't worry, the Pilgrims RINSED.

Up in the Arctic, there is barely enough fuel to cook food, let alone melt snow to clean SEAL BLUBBER off the dinner dishes. So after a meal, some people used to pee into the dishpan to produce the hot "water" needed to wash up.

Other people have used pee to wash themselves. The Inuit cleaned up in steam baths made by peeing on hot rocks in enclosed tents. And in parts of India and East Africa where water is scarce or polluted, people still bathe in cow urine.

A few centuries ago, the ladies of England and France loved the way urine gave their skin a FRESH GLOW. Many of them peed on their hands to soften them. Others used puppy pee instead.

Here in the United States of the twenty-first century, we don't pee on our hands—except by mistake. Instead, we let laboratories pull the MAGIC INGREDIENT out of urine that smoothes and moistens our skin. Then, when it's safely called "urea," we put it into our creams and lotions.

PEE SOUP

The Chinook Indian tribe used to make "CHINOOK OLIVES" by soaking acorns in pee for five months. European bakers used pee to help their bread rise before they discovered yeast. And some Africans still mix cow urine into their milk.

Butterflies sip nectar from flowers, but they flutter over to pee-soaked leaves and puddles any chance they get. Urine is a butterfly's best source of VITAMINS.

Reindeer love the stuff because they don't have many other ways to get salt. In fact, when Siberian men want to catch their reindeer to hook them up to their sleds, they just go outside and unfasten their pants. The reindeer rush right over.

The Inuit used to catch wild reindeer by covering the top of a pit with thin slabs of ice. Then they would pee in a line leading up to the trap and add a couple of EXTRA SPLASHES on top. The reindeer couldn't believe their good luck—until they fell into the pit.

During their long months of hibernation, bears don't pee at all. They RECYCLE. Their bodies convert their pee into protein and use it as food.

IT'S A TRAP!

WEE BEASTIES

Skin softener, heart medicine, a weapon in the battle against global warming—pee is clearly a help to us throughout our lives. But did you know that its usefulness begins even before we are born?

While we grow in our mothers' bellies, we *FLOAT* in a sac of fluid. As we get bigger, the sac gets bigger and the amount of liquid doubles. Toward the end of our time in there, most of that liquid is urine.

HEY, WE HAD TO PEE SOMEWHERE.

And it's good that we did; this pee helped us grow. We swallowed it and peed it out, over and over again. It exercised our lungs and windpipes so we could eat and breathe for the rest of our lives.

Clearly this was a very important routine. But it's no wonder we're ready to get out of there after nine months!

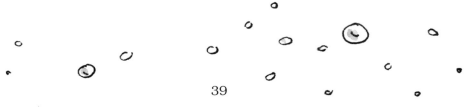

IN 1917, ARTIST MARCEL DUCHAMP SIGNED A URINAL AND PUT IT IN AN ART EXHIBIT. RECENTLY A POLL OF 500 EXPERTS NAMED IT THE MOST INFLUENTIAL WORK OF MODERN ART. • LONG AGO, ALCHEMISTS TRIED TO FIND GOLD IN PEE. THEY THOUGHT THIS METAL WAS RESPONSIBLE FOR PEE'S YELLOW COLOR. • A PEE-POWERED PAPER BATTERY HAS BEEN DEVELOPED. IT'S NOT READY TO RUN A LAPTOP BUT CAN GENERATE ENOUGH ELECTRICITY FOR A SMALL EMERGENCY CELL PHONE. • BIRDS HAVE ONLY ONE OPENING TO GET RID OF THEIR WASTE, SO THEIR PEE AND POOP COMES OUT TOGETHER. • DOCTORS HAD SUCH A SMALL AMOUNT OF PENICILLIN FOR ITS FIRST TEST IN HUMANS THAT THEY COLLECTED WHAT WAS LEFT OF IT FROM THE PATIENT'S PEE AND GAVE IT TO HIM AGAIN. • INSTEAD OF RETURNING TO THE SHIP TO PEE DURING A SPACEWALK, ASTRONAUTS WEAR DIAPERS THAT CAN ABSORB OVER A QUART OF LIQUID. • INDIA'S FORMER PRIME MINISTER MORARJI DESAI LIVED TO BE NINETY-NINE YEARS OLD. HE SAID HE OWED HIS GOOD HEALTH TO DRINKING A PINT OF HIS OWN URINE EACH DAY. • IN SINGAPORE, NOT FLUSHING PUBLIC TOILETS IS A CRIME. UNDERCOVER AGENTS LURK IN RESTROOMS TO HAND OUT FINES. • NATIVE AUSTRALIANS BELIEVED THAT OCEANS WERE CREATED BY A GOD WHO, DISGUSTED WITH PEOPLE'S WICKEDNESS, TRIED TO DROWN THE WORLD WITH HIS PEE. • THE GREEK PHILOSOPHER ARISTOTLE TRIED TO CURE HIS BALDNESS BY RUBBING HIS HEAD WITH GOAT URINE. • A SURVEY SHOWS THAT 42 PERCENT OF PEOPLE FOLD THEIR TOILET PAPER